MEET ME AT HARVEST MOON

Also From Wilde Press

Rose Red by Naomi Bloom
TwoSpan Time by Rita Chun
This Cursed Death by Teya Sorenson
The Neural Network by Madeline Gregorski
Lisoyid by Karina Jha
Always Winter by Madeline Monroe
Shrine Maiden by DS Oswald
Fame and Other Candies by Haley Souders
Something More by Audrey Iocca
Letters to Space by Valentine
The Destruction of One, Penelope Evans by Isabella Rodrigues
Rootlines by Kelsey Day
Seat of the Soul by Clarah Grossman
To Help and to Heal by Katie Lacadie
The Biography of an Unknown Soldier by Andi Smith
Para Curarte by Ximena Delgado
Thoughts & Prayers by Owen Elphick
As Most Things Are by Hannah Kelly
Bird Folk by Antonio Weathers
Here, There, & Everywhere by Rebekah Scarborough
Catfish & Other Dead Things by Genna Coleman
Haunting at St. Peter's Academy by Marissa Secreto
Beautiful Homeland Mother Earth by Patrick Groleau
Wandering & Other Stories by Melissa Close
Under Floorboard, Under Skin by Allison Rassman
Butterflies Behind Glass & Other Stories by Kyle Labe
Middlelands by Al Reitz
Lo Siento Miguel by Andrew Siañez-De La O
Memories of an Old World by Julio Cesar Villegas
Bruises by Elizabeth Capot
Gay by May by David Carliner
These Thoughts That Hold Us by Sarah Cummings
To the Strangers, from Far Away by Bailey Tamayo
Venetian Blue and Other Obscene Colors by Sahalie Angell Martin
When the Gardner Has Left by Kieran Collier
The Incredible Superfets by Michael J. Schuck
Hypergraphia by Brenna Kleiman *The World From Jar* by Rebecca Crandall
Animal Magnetism by Meaghan O'Brien
Only Show in Town by Bobby Crawford

MEET ME AT HARVEST MOON

Callan Whitley

Wilde Press | Boston

Published by Wilde Press, Boston, MA
Trade paperback ISBN 978-1-957965-27-7
Cover design by Anya Getschel
Cover concept and illustration by Elisabeth Grass
Interior design by Anya Getschel
Interior illustrations by Anya Getschel, Ella Mastroianni, Isabelle McMahan, and Eva Windler
Typefaces used are Bodoni Ornaments, Caraque, and Garamond Premier Pro
Printed by Flagship Press, North Andover, MA
All proceeds from this book go to Reach Out and Read Massachusetts

*To my mom, dad, and grandparents, for shipping me off
to Boston to live out my dreams.*

And to Sophia and Dev, who make life all colors at once.

CONTENTS

One ❁ Mouse the Cat *1*

Two ❁ Lenny's Very Peculiar Wish *7*

Three ❁ The Bicycle Ride of a Lifetime *15*

Four ❁ A Laundry Malfunction Sends Us
Plummeting to Our Deaths *21*

Five ❁ Our Harvest Moon Rendezvous *27*

Six ❁ Franky *35*

Seven ❁ The Sweetest Apple *43*

Eight ❁ All The Colors at Once *53*

Nine ❁ Goodbye *59*

CHAPTER ONE
MOUSE THE CAT

This year, the cat in the yellow raincoat and I went fishing for the Harvest Moon. We met at dusk on the rocky lake, where the September air was crisp and crimson.

I rode in on my bicycle and heard the crunch of fallen leaves beneath the rickety wheels. Gazing out to the moon, he was waiting for me on a rock at the edge of the lake. And, indeed, it was a splendid sight. The glowing orb looked like it had been dipped in honey as it loomed over the night sky.

"Hello, Ghosty," the cat grumbled, still looking out.

I sighed, propping my wooden bike on the willow tree. "You know, I've never really been fond of that nickname."

"Tell me that when you stop tripping over your own sheet."

"I see that you've taken my suggestion to work on your manners."

The cat huffed and puffed. "Manners! What a dreadfully human notion. Like monotony. And taxes. All very unnecessary," he murmured and hopped off the rock.

"Whatever you say, Mouse." That earned an eye roll.

Mouse was a very peculiar cat in that he was not very catlike at all. For one, the tabby stood and walked on his furry hind legs. For as long as I had known him, he wore a bright yellow, rubbery raincoat with three ruby-red buttons down the front. He always insisted on wearing the hood up so that it framed his chubby, round face. It fit him like an oversized flared peacoat, with his bushy tail sticking out the back. He was not very tall, but what he lacked in height, he most certainly made up in attitude. That was to say, Mouse called the shots.

"Besides, I'm not really human, am I?" I asked and shrugged.

I was a sheet ghost. A rarity around here, sure, but not completely unheard of. We were kind of like the stray dogs of this world. We wandered around these lands, lost and befuddled. But, occasionally, someone grew tired of us showing up at their doorstep with puppy dog eyes and took us in. That's what Mouse did for me, despite his aversion to dogs. And helping people. And people.

I should've mentioned that instead of a crisp white linen, I'm a tattered flower sheet. I think that's ridiculous, by the way. I'm already dead, which is kind of a low blow from the universe in and of itself. But to make matters worse, I'm stuck forever as a chalky, white sheet. It's decorated with daisies like a grandma's quilt set. Ugh, not exactly the macho look I was going for. You know, whenever I figure out who decides what sheet a dead person gets, I'm going to have some choice words with them!

(I will not, under any circumstances, be having choice words with anyone. I am actually not very macho, and confrontation makes me sneeze. My choice of words would probably be: *Hello, sir. Do I call you sir? Sorry, sir. I like the sheet, sir, very macho.*)

"No, but you still reek like a human," Mouse leaned in, making a show of sniffing me. "Mhm. Yes, definitely human. They all smell the same. Like a failed entrepreneurial project. Or a suburban mom going door to door selling overpriced skincare products. Very pungent," he said with a sigh. "Now, why are you late for this very important fishing appointment?"

"I was improving the final product!" I said, waving my wooden fishing rod in the air.

Mouse stood on his tippy-toes, inspecting the modified fishing pole I had constructed for our expedition. He didn't bother to hide his skepticism as he eyed my invention.

"Are you sure this is going to work?"

"Don't you trust me?"

"Cats don't trust anyone," he announced plainly. "That's how we've come to get nine lives."

"Very cynical, Mouse. Not a good look on you, if I do say so myself."

"Well, let's just hope your tinkering will prove itself useful."

"Mouse, would you please be quiet like a—"

"Don't you dare say it—"

"—mouse while I set this up," I retorted, readying the fishing rod.

Around the shore, fireflies buzzed in and out like warm, floating candlelight. Everything seemed to be alive tonight. The earth was bountiful in full autumnal bloom. An array of sunflowers, red chrysanthemums, and yellow daisies lined the tallgrass area of the lake. They swayed softly, dancing to the whisper of the wind.

And, of course, there was the moon. The star of the show, and the reason we were here tonight. Hovering above the lake, it looked like a ginormous pumpkin. The Harvest equinox had drawn it so close to land that I felt like I could reach out and touch it. It hung low, dipping into the surface of the water like a mother kissing her child goodnight.

Tonight was the Harvest Moon, the first full moon closest to the autumnal equinox. When the days finally collided with September, when the leaves turned yellow and the nights grew long, there was believed to be a special kind of magic in the air.

And there was something special about the moon on that very night. There was a legend that for the folks brave enough to journey to the top of the moon, the Spirit of the Harvest had the power to grant the voyager one wish.

"Ready to see her?" Mouse asked with a glimmer in his eyes only a true adventure could bring out.

Her. Francine.

I squeezed my black holes (eyes, as commonly referred to by humans). I saw her: a girl with sun-soaked hair and freckles like dirt.

That's why we were going, Mouse and I.

A sheet ghost and a cat in a yellow raincoat, off to see a girl on the moon.

CHAPTER TWO
LENNY'S VERY PECULIAR WISH

Mouse and I first learned about the Harvest Moon at a bear's birthday bash.

Mouse was in no mood to celebrate.

"Well, who do we have here? Mr. Mouse, dapper as always. Though, I'm not sure rain is on the forecast, little one." The bear in the rainbow-striped birthday hat had a wide smile, brown, scratchy fur, and a deep southern twang. He swung the door open with a goofy grin almost immediately after Mouse had knocked.

"And you've brought a friend. Oh, that's excellent," the bear said looking down at me. His wide eyes jolted as he took in my sheet. Like I said, we're not that common around here.

"Ah, you scared me!" He hollered and slapped his brown, bulging belly.

Mouse and I gave him a blank stare.

"... 'Cause you're a ghost," the bear added, obviously unaware that his joke did not land. In fact, the joke didn't even make it in the air. It exploded before the plane took off.

"Well, I'm Lenny. It's a real pleasure to meet me," he boasted and tipped his birthday hat to me. "And what might you call yourself, li'l ghost?"

I cleared my throat. "I'm Ghosty."

Lenny tilted his head quizzically at my daisy sheet.

"Oh, that's nice." His southern drawl was thick and burly. "Little on the nose, isn't it?"

I sneezed once and then a second time. It was a nervous quirk of mine in unpleasant situations like this. My sheet always flew up with the motion.

In truth, Ghosty was just a nickname Mouse teased me with that eventually stuck. And I was happy it did. There was a reason sheet ghosts are treated like the stray dogs of this world—we don't really have a home to go to. You see, we wake up here without a memory from our past life. No recollections of who we were or what we did. That was why we wandered around this world so lost. We were trying to remember.

But there was something strange about my case. I *did* remember. At least, a little bit. When I shut my eyes and tried to picture the one memory I had, it was murky like a dream. I could see a young girl, around the age of twelve. She had golden hair and a missing tooth. It was like I was seeing her through a weird, greenish film. Then my arm was stretched out, and I was reaching toward something bright red.

I knew her name was Francine. Of course, there was no way I could've known that, but I did.

It completely defied the logic of sheet ghosts in this world, but I remembered her. Mouse said it's a good thing. Because sheet ghosts are stuck here without memories, he said that they can never find their peace. But I had a memory. I had a chance to find peace.

Now, I wasn't exactly sure what *peace* even meant. But it was my understanding that if I was somehow able to remember my past, I could find it. That's what Mouse said, at least. If sheet ghosts could remember their old lives, they could move on to the next one.

"Yes, speaking of noses, what is that god-awful smell?" Mouse asked as he stuck his head in the doorway to sniff for a culprit.

"Oh well, they're moonpies, silly! You know, for the Harvest Festival today!" Lenny started talking out of the side of his mouth. "Well, I'll be honest with you folks, I did run out of moon a couple of days ago. But I had fish, so it's more of a fish pie. Except I had a little too much flour, so it's more of a cake situation—"

"I'm begging you to stop." Mouse glowered at him.

I hadn't a clue what he was talking about. *Moonpies? Harvest Festival?*

As Lenny beckoned us into his cottage, he was quick to slap pointy birthday hats onto both of us. Mouse immediately ripped his off. I had to float around very carefully to keep mine from slipping off my sheet. Not only was Lenny a little too plump for his own tiny home, but he had about as much grace as a bulldozer. As he made his way through, his belly and behind bumped into pots, pans, chairs, you name it. When he finally squeezed himself into the main living room with us in tow, he excitedly introduced us to some of the other party guests who looked exactly as thrilled to be there as Mouse was. There was a donkey, a scarecrow, and a gigantic bat; all barely fit in the house at all.

"Y'all can put the gifts on the table! That's what everyone else has been doing," Lenny announced in front of a wobbly, wooden table with not a single birthday present in sight. Quickly, he shot us a look with a pointed paw. "And just 'cause y'all came together don't mean a combined gift, alright? Have some manners."

I felt the beginning of a sneeze. A birthday present! We had completely forgotten to bring him a gift.

"Lenny, I'm so sorry! We don't have a present for you."

Lenny whipped his head around. For a moment, the burly bear was no longer flashing his game-show-host smile. He tilted his head, absolutely flabbergasted.

"And what might you mean by that, li'l ghost?"

"Um," I swallowed. "Well, we decided very last minute to come, and it must've slipped our minds! We're terribly sorry—"

"But it's my birthday."

"Well, I know that." Sneeze.

Lenny gave me a dumbstruck stare. Blinked. Then suddenly he chuckled. I'd never heard such a boisterous laugh given with dead, wide eyes. "No worries, li'l ghost. Can't say it don't hurt my feelings, but I'm a big bear! Anyway, I suppose you can just bring me them tomorrow!"

Mouse sighed. "We will not be bringing you a gift tomorrow."

"Alright, alright, Mouse, you cheeky li'l cat!" He gave us a deathly serious expression. "You can bring me a couple to make up for your grievances—"

Mouse sighed. "We will not be bringing you a gift tomorrow."

Before Mouse could interject, I did: "We absolutely will! Or, you know, next year we can bring you a really big one?"

Mouse rolled his eyes like he could not be more bored of this conversation. "Lenny has a bit of a unique birthday situation."

I gave Mouse a puzzled look. "What do you mean?"

"Every day is his birthday," Mouse replied.

"What?"

Mouse's yellow eyes leered at Lenny. "Care to explain?"

"That is extremely personal, Mr. Mouse." To his credit, Lenny put on one stellar performance of pretending like he did not want to talk about it.

I redirected my attention back to Mouse. "So you're saying . . . he was born every single day of the year? That doesn't make any sense."

Mouse shook his head. "No, just that every day is his birthday."

"Huh?" I said again.

"Pretty nifty, ain't it?" Lenny puffed out his cheeks and looked like he was on the verge of passing out with excitement.

"How'd you manage that?" I asked.

"Well, that's very confidential, li'l ghost."

Back to Mouse (I was getting whiplash between the two of them): "How did he do it?"

"He took a trip to the moon—"

"Okay, okay!" Lenny shot his paws up. "Well, if the story is gonna be told, I might as well tell it 'cause no offense Mouse, but you're not someone I'd really call an entertainer." Lenny threw himself in a chair at the kitchen table. When he took a deep breath, it reminded me of an actor preparing for a big role right before the curtains went up. Actually, I think that was exactly what was happening.

"Well, I took a little trip to the moon." Lenny wiggled his eyebrows and leaned forward. "But it was a very peculiar kind of moon, you see. They call it a Harvest Moon."

I perked up. "Like the Harvest Festival? That thing you said is happening today?"

"Well, yes, li'l ghost. They pack a brain into that sheet of yours? Didn't you see the moon outside on 'yer way here? It's the first full moon after the equinox. It glows all orange like a great big pumpkin. They say the Spirit brings all sorts of neat things to us this time of year, like luck and wealth. And of course"—*theatrical pause*—"magic.

"But it's a very special kind of magic. There's an old folklore that gets passed between us bears, very confidential stuff. But you look like a face I can trust, li'l ghost." He continued in a whisper: "Us bears think the Harvest Moon has the power to grant wishes, 'yer hear? So a couple Harvest Moons ago, I took it upon myself to investigate this li'l tale. And what do you know, when I got to the moon, there was this funky kind of water in a big crater. Like a dreamy little pool. At first I panicked." He paused and looked between us. "I didn't pack my trunks. But then I was like, what the heck? A bear only goes swimming on the moon once.

"When I was in the pool, I suddenly got this tinkle in my toes. Them bears are always saying the magic of the moon is supposed to show you whatever your heart desires. I felt like I could ask my magical Jacuzzi for anything I wanted in the whole wide world, and it would give it to me. Suddenly, I was very overwhelmed with all the potential wishes. What was a bear to do? So I sat there for quite a long time. And then I started to sweat 'cause I was worried I would miss my birthday. Which is, of course, my very favorite day of the year." He clapped his paws together. "And then it struck me! I'll make every day my birthday! So we can all celebrate the very best day every single day! You see, it was really more of a wish for everyone. I'm what they call a champion of the people—"

"And this wish thing—it worked?" I interrupted.

"Well, we're here at my birthday party, aren't we?"

I peered around at the strange guests in the cottage. The more I thought about it, the more they looked like a group of hostages held against their will with birthday hats strapped to their heads.

"So . . ." I said, piecing it all together. "You went to the moon. And that's where you got all the stuff to make the moonpies?"

"Fish cakes," Lenny quickly corrected me. "Anyway, enough of this chitchat! Y'all wanna play pin the tail on the donkey?" Lenny raised his paws up in defense with a sudden serious look. "Just kidding! Glen didn't like that very much last year."

The donkey to my left made a grunt.

My mind started to race. Did the Harvest Moon really have the power to grant wishes? How does one even *get* to the moon?

And then I thought of Francine. She must be the missing piece to the puzzle, the key to finding out who I was before. If I could somehow talk to her, maybe she could help me remember. I could find my peace.

As Lenny gathered us around the table with a moonpie with a candle stuck in it and forced us to sing him "Happy Birthday," I came up with a plan. If this goon could make a wish on the moon, what's to stop me? I could somehow make a wish to see her again.

I leaned over and whispered to Mouse, "Got any plans for tonight?"

"Other than trying to forget what I've been subjected to this past hour, no. Why?" he wondered.

"Mouse, you and I are going to the moon."

CHAPTER THREE
THE BICYCLE RIDE OF A LIFETIME

❀ ❀ ❀

Now, you've got to wind it up real nice and smooth," Mouse said. He pointed at my fishing rod and then to the gigantic, hovering moon.

"I think I can do it. I did make it myself, you know."

My genius plan to get to the moon involved a fishing rod, one rickety bicycle, and a lot of luck. It was a little crazy, sure, but we didn't have much time. In the hours since Lenny's birthday party, we had been scrambling to figure out how to make it up there. Phase one began with me casting a fishing line up to the moon. Easy enough, right?

I wound it up, throwing the pole behind my shoulder, not before almost jabbing Mouse in the eye. He jumped out of the way and made a very un-Mouse-like meow. Like a spooked, wet cat. Except he was, of course, Mouse. And not very catlike at all. A very confusing fellow.

"Good first try. Except if I had one critique, maybe try not to take one of my eyeballs with you next time."

"You sure? I've always thought an eye patch would complement your anger management issues quite nicely. You could be like a rabid-alleyway-pirate cat."

"Oh, you've decided to be cheeky again. How lovely," Mouse cooed.

Again, I tossed the fishing pole behind me, carefully sidestepping the grumpy animal with claws next to me. I put as much strength into it as I could, casting the line past the lake and high into the sky. The line jumped from the pole as if it was in slow motion and reached toward the moon. It should be impossible, but the Harvest had drawn the moon so close to land that the line made it to the surface. I felt it grab onto the moon, hooking into one of the craters like a fish's mouth. The line formed a diagonal tightrope, a slope leading up to the nighttime sky.

"Nice one, Ghosty!" Mouse announced, clapping his paws like a little kid.

We watched in awe as the moon's touch transformed the line. Like a fire traveling slowly down a match, the fishing line became golden.

I tugged the handle a couple of times to make sure it was tight. Together, we grabbed the end of the line and wrapped it around the trunk of the willow tree to secure it. Mouse wobbled over, wheeling my bicycle to the start of our makeshift tightrope. I raised my bike and put it on the beginning of the line so it was angled upward and balanced on the tightrope.

Phase two might've been Mouse's least favorite. He reluctantly held up his tiny front legs with an exaggerated sigh. I lifted him up and plopped him into the bike's woven basket. I gave him two pats on the head for good measure. Mouse did not like it when I gave him two pats on the head for good measure.

"Alright, alright," he hissed, shoving me off. He sat crisscrossed in the basket, grabbing onto both sides of the carrier. "Let's get going, Ghosty!"

"Wait," I said, looking around. My sheet scrunched with the motion. "I have to do something first."

I didn't know much about human girls. Or humans, for that matter. But everyone likes flowers, right?

I bent over and plucked a few yellow daisies from the ground. Pretty but humble.

Mouse shook his head when I floated back. "Oh god, sheet ghosts and their sentimentality."

"Mouse, I am the only sheet ghost you know," I replied, floating up to the bicycle's seat.

"Yes. But you're dripping wet with good intentions and big dreams. So I've decided to stereotype you all as moon-eyed romantics."

"Hey, I'm not being romantic. Just polite. Not that I would expect you to understand what that means," I said.

"Mhm," he huffed.

I glanced down at the bundle of flowers I'd shoved in the basket of the bike next to Mouse. "Do you not like them?"

"For your little girlfriend or for me? Ghosty, I'm flattered, but flowers aren't exactly—"

"She's not my girlfriend!" I uttered quickly. "She's… She's my…"

"She's your . . ." Mouse asked.

"My neighbor," I clarified. Again, I didn't know how to explain it, but I just had a feeling. I knew she was my neighbor.

"Hurry!" Mouse exclaimed, pointing to the quickly darkening sky. As the sun abandoned the earth, the moon began to shine brighter. We didn't know how much time we had.

I pushed on the bike's pedals and propelled us forward. I should probably explain here that I, being a sheet ghost, obviously don't have any visible elongated limbs. But they were there all the same, invisibly pedaling the bike.

Same thing with my arms. It was like they were there, underneath my sheet, but not really *there*.

I don't know. I don't think too much about it. You probably don't want to either.

We began our slow climb up the mountain of the glistening tightrope. I kept my smile to myself as Mouse leaned forward, paws gripping the front of the basket. It seemed like even grumpy, old cats were not immune to the beauty of autumn.

I looked down below us. The light of the moon was reflected in the dark water of the lake, twinkling like a pool of blazing firelight. A swirl of bright light and orange hues ripped through the soft cascades of the water. When the wheels of the bicycle contacted the line, bits of starlight sputtered off and fell into the lake.

Our own images shined back at us, and what an odd sight it was. Mouse's raincoat was squeaky yellow like a rubber duck in the water. His fluffy tail stuck straight out behind him in anticipation.

"Ghosty! Look!" Mouse exclaimed, pointing to our right.

A red and white-striped hot-air balloon floated upward against the yellow stars of the night sky. It glided across the horizon, reaching toward the moon. The basket-woven gondola gently swayed underneath. Inside was an all-too-excited bear with an all-too-familiar birthday hat.

"Oh, you've got to be kidding me," Mouse groaned.

"Well, I guess that solves the great mystery of how Lenny made it to the moon," I said.

As we climbed closer and closer, we spotted all the clever ways others had found to make it to the Harvest Moon Festival. I was startled by three round water bubbles that were clear with a bluish tint. They appeared as though they'd been plucked from the ocean. When I peered closer, I saw huge goldfish inside each of the bubbles. Their image was distorted, like I had my forehead pressed against a fishbowl. They wiggled and swam in place, floating slowly to the moon. How's that for a ride?

I didn't have much time to gawk at the family of fish before I was almost thrown off-balance as a bat soared above us. It was the size of a small dragon and pitch black, save for white pointy ears on top. It took its time, gracefully weaving in and out of the stars. On his back was a tiny squirrel carrying as many acorns as he could manage, leading the charge like a soldier in battle.

"We're almost there," Mouse announced. His voice was soft as he stared wide-eyed at the marvel of the moon.

I looked up, making out the moon's bumpy texture, the crooks and crevices of its craters. The soft glow, akin to molten gold, embraced the night sky like a warm hug.

"Yes, indeed we are."

CHAPTER FOUR
A Laundry Malfunction Sends Us Plummeting to Our Deaths

The longer I squinted at the moon, the more I began to feel very itchy. Suddenly, it didn't seem so beautiful anymore. It was too blinding, too big, and too bright. The Harvest had flooded everything with light, making me feel quite dizzy.

I looked down at my sheet, and my black holes bulged out. Quickly, I snapped my head up.

"Is my sheet wrinkled?"

Mouse turned back and looked at me, nodding succinctly. "Most regrettably so."

"Oh my goodness!" I started to sweat. Then I glanced down and realized I could not sweat because I was a sheet ghost. Sometimes I forget. But it was very stressful all the same!

"I know. You can't imagine how upset I am about it," Mouse droned.

"Oh no," I breathed out, pulling and yanking on my sheet, trying to smooth it. I started to see everything in microscopic detail.

I noticed the girly daisies on the linen, the frilled edges, and the ratty holes where moths had used my sheet as an afternoon snack.

Then I gazed at the daisies in the basket. "And these flowers—they're ridiculous, aren't they? Just go ahead and tell me. I know they are."

"They're ridiculous."

"How could you say that to me right now?!"

Mouse rolled his eyes. "Calm down. Your sheet is starting to look like an airplane vomit bag."

"Oh, and my hair," I babbled, grabbing the top of my head. "It must look like a bird's nest!"

"Ghosty, get a grip! You don't even have hair!"

"Right!" I was relieved for just a second. "Well, that just makes matters even worse, actually!" I sneezed once and then a second time.

"Might I say, you're quite full of anxiety for someone who is already dead. I mean, really." He sighed, waving one of his paws in the air. "What more do you have to lose?"

"My dignity, my sense of self, my peace of mind . . ." I listed off rapidly.

He considered this for a moment. "All very trivial things in the cat world."

"We have to turn back!" I announced, halting my pedaling and suspending us in midair. The momentum launched Mouse forward and he let loose a raucous meow. It forced him to grab onto the basket to steady himself.

"It's all wrong; everything is wrong!" I sneezed.

"What on earth are you doing?" Mouse gasped, scrambling to face me.

"We're turning this train around!" I declared.

The pedals start to fly backward beneath me, like a hamster running on a wheel. If the stakes weren't so high, it would've actually been pretty funny. But seeing as the meaning of my entire existence was hanging in the balance, maybe not.

This was something I was pretty sure Mouse agreed with. As the bicycle zipped toward the lake, Mouse waved his paws up and down wildly in front of my face. "Stop that!"

"We can come back another time!" I sputtered. "Yes, another time would be good. I have plans tonight, anyway. Doesn't work with my schedule. Very busy!"

"You have absolutely no plans! I am your only friend!" Mouse cried out.

He leaped forward to grab onto me with his arms, wrapping himself around my head. My life flashed before my eyes in a blur of a yellow raincoat, bared teeth, and irate meows. We scrambled as he reached for the handle to halt the break. I swatted him away. In retrospect, this was not something you should do to a cat with known anger issues while his claws are flailing about. His meows sounded like he was caught in a blender as we raced backward.

"AHHH!" He screamed.

"AHHHHHH!" I yelled.

"Why," he puffed out, "are *you* screaming?"

"Well, it just kind of feels like a roller coaster, and you know how queasy I get!" I yelped, frantically feeling around my sheet. "Good heavens, I forgot to bring Dramamine—"

"You idiot! Sheet ghosts can't take Dramamine!"

"Well, they should really make these things more accessible for everyone—"

"Ghosty," he called. He rearranged himself so we were face to face, and he was grabbing onto my sheet. "I swear if you weren't already dead, I'd kill you!"

I sneezed. "Noted. Okay. Thank you."

"Ghosty!"

"You'll be fine!" I screeched. "I hear cats always stick the landing!"

"Slam the brakes!"

I shook my head rapidly. "I can't!"

"Why not!"

"Because what if she's not there?" I yelled back.

"What?!" Mouse screamed, barely able to hear me over the harsh whistle of the wind as we plummeted.

I slammed the brakes on the pedal. Our tires screeched as the bike abruptly halted along the tightrope, halfway between the moon and the base of the willow tree. Catching my breath, I nervously peeked over at Mouse, who had ended up hanging onto the button of the basket's handles like a sloth on a branch.

I gasped through breaths of air. "Because what if she's not there? What if she doesn't want to see me?"

Mouse regained his composure, crawling up to sit in the basket. He looked at me from the hood of his raincoat like he was two seconds away from slicing my sheet in half, his green eyes blazing. Yet, as soon as he saw my face, something in his manner changed. His expression softened a bit, and his whiskers turned down. I sneezed.

"What?" he asked.

"I've just . . . I don't know . . . I've been thinking. Well, why would she want to see me, anyway? I'm . . . I'm not anything." I looked down. "Just a sheet ghost who sneezes a lot and has no hair."

"The hair thing really bothers you, doesn't it?"

"Yeah, well, it's a tough loss." I sniffled. "I imagine it was very fluffy and soft."

"I'm sure it was," he mused.

We sat there in silence for a bit while the moon hovered over us.

"Well, my friend, I can't say I've met a lot of sheet ghosts, or any for that matter. But I've lived a lot of lives. Seven, to be exact. And I think this is one of my favorites. Because . . ." Mouse sighed. Indeed, it really was paining him to be this emotional. "Because I met you. A sheet ghost who sneezes a lot and doesn't have any hair."

I looked back up to him. "Hey," I realized. "I didn't know you were on your seventh life!"

"Cats don't trust anyone with sensitive information. That's how we've come to get this far."

"And?"

Mouse eyed me. "And . . . maybe I can make this one exception."

I laughed. "Well, what are we waiting for?"

He rolled his eyes and situated himself in the basket. I took a deep breath.

Pushing on the pedals again, I began our slow ascent.

To the Harvest Moon we go.

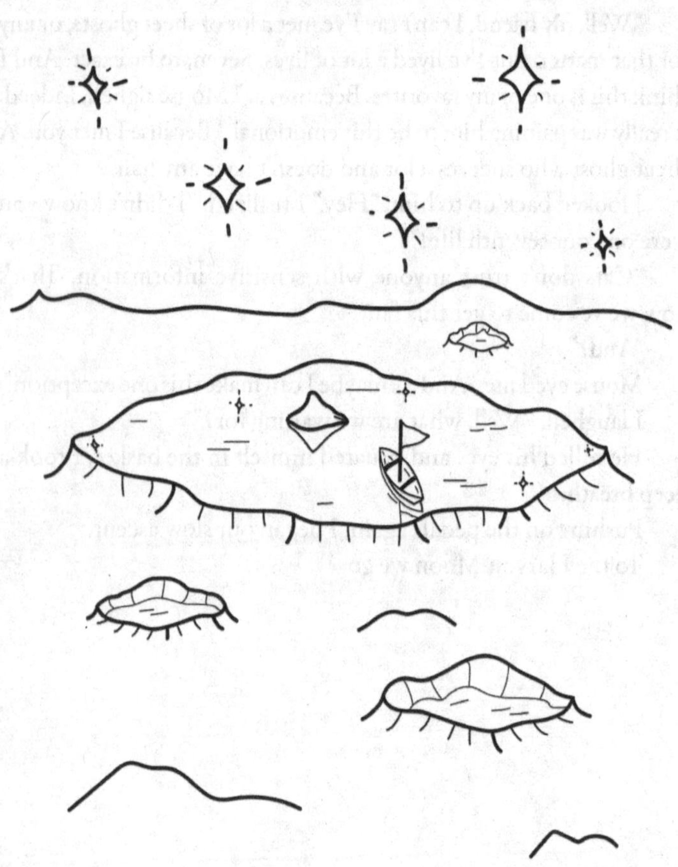

CHAPTER FIVE
OUR HARVEST MOON RENDEZVOUS

When we arrived at the Harvest Festival on the moon, it was quite a spectacle. Mouse and I jumped off the bicycle. I stifled a laugh as Mouse wobbled on his feet, trying to get his footing. It was like we had found ourselves on top of a big, orange bouncy ball. The citrus moon was rubbery, rounded, and sloped.

Red and white-striped tents lined the rolling hills of the craters like a grand carnival, pumping out the sweet scent of apple treats. The slopes were filled with the crops of the season—giant acorns, sheaves of wheat, and towering husks of corn. A plentiful pumpkin patch was lit by the glow of a thousand tiny fairies. Scarecrows in patchwork overalls teetered in between the crowds, carrying bunches of sunflowers to bargain with the chattering spectators. A Ferris wheel stood tall against the backdrop of the twilight sky, casting a yellow hue over the festival.

It seemed like the festival wasn't just a well-kept secret among the community of bears. Creatures from every nook and cranny had come here to celebrate—prancing deer, wise owls with glasses, and bunny rabbits with tall ears had all gathered on the moon.

"Moonpies! Get your moonpies!" a red fox to the left of us shouted to the bustling crowd. She was wearing a frilly apron with a box full of pastries strapped to her neck.

"Hey," I nudged Mouse. "I guess Lenny was right about those moonpies. Maybe he isn't so loony after all."

"I wouldn't be so sure of that," Mouse retorted quickly. I followed his line of sight, where the goon stood next to a tent shoveling moonpie after moonpie into his mouth. He had not ditched his pointy birthday hat, but the bear was dressed to impress in a red, polka-dotted bow tie. When Lenny spotted us, he eagerly waved us over.

Mouse and I exchanged a defeated look. It was too late to make a run for it, so we trudged over.

"Now, I *thought* that was y'all on the bicycle," Lenny hollered with cheeks full of moonpie, slapping Mouse on the shoulder when we greeted him.

I saw Mouse flare his nostrils.

"That was us," I said quickly, trying to diffuse the tension.

"Brilliant! Now, how's that for a Harvest Moon rendezvous? But, um, level with me here, li'l ghost." He bent down so we were eye to eye—or black hole, in my case.

"Yes?"

"Not that I don't admire arriving with style, but why couldn't you just float up here?"

Mouse glared at me as if to say: *We could've just done* that *all along!*

I cleared my throat. "Well, um, didn't think about that."

Lenny nodded. "Well, we can't all be fine intellectuals like myself."

Just then, the family of goldfish in the water bubbles floated above us like clouds, cleverly avoiding the crowd. I saw Lenny's eyes go wide with an idea.

"Hey li'l ghost, mind if I borrow that handy dandy fishing rod of yours? There's gonna be a huge demand for my specialty fish pies at tomorrow's birthday party."

"Not that a cat is in any position to advocate for fish, but I don't think they would enjoy being turned into pastries," Mouse pointed out.

"Alright Mr. Mouse, but you're gonna have the masses to answer to."

As Lenny ushered us through the crowd, we followed the strum of folk music. When we stumbled upon the heart of the festival, a band of woodland creatures was leading the crowd in a foot-stomping dance. At the center of the musical escapade, a raccoon played the fiddle with gusto. His paws danced across the strings, creating a lively tune that echoed through the hills of the moon. A squirrel with a bushy tail plucked the string of a banjo while an orange fox shook a tambourine.

Front and center at the microphone, a bear in a top hat with a red feather led the ensemble, adding a toe-tapping rhythm to the jam.

Next to me, Lenny's good mood had turned sour. "Gosh dangit!"

"Something the matter?" I asked him.

"Now what the heck is Uncle Rick doing here?"

Mouse gestured to the lead singer. "You know him?"

Lenny puffed his chest out. "Oh, boy do I! He used to be a mighty fine gentleman, let me tell you. Then he joined a band and all of a sudden he's Mr. No-Lenny-I'm-Not-Gonna-Come-To-Every-Single-One-Of-Your-Birthday-Parties. And Mr. Also-Your-Moonpies-Taste-Like-Fish! Good grief!"

"Well, some people just think the whole world revolves around themselves," Mouse quipped.

"It is downright distasteful." Lenny shook his head. "And my moonpies are cream of the crop! Crème de la crème. He can't take that away from me."

I glanced around. Through the sea of dancers, I could spot another sheet ghost. Their sheet was dark blue with white stars. I waved to them as if to say: *Wow, nice sheet!* In response, they only slumped in their linen. *Huh,* I thought. *They seem so sad. I wonder why.*

"So is everyone here to cast a wish?" Mouse asked Lenny curiously, pulling me away from the blue sheet ghost.

"Well, yes and no. The festival's about much more than that. See those things over there?" He pointed to a group of bears huddled around a tent, readying a collection of lanterns.

"At the end of the festival, everyone releases a lantern into the air. I reckon it's supposed to symbolize being grateful for the crops and letting go of past worries—all that jazz. Besides, 'ya only get one wish per year. And trust me, the Jacuzzi cannot be fooled with a mustache and a pair of sunglasses. Better men have tried."

I nudged Mouse again. "So what are you going to wish for?"

Mouse scrunched his nose, suddenly squirmy. "None of your business."

"Tell me."

"I am curious as to what you think 'none of your business' implies."

"Well, I'll just have to make something up in my mind. Hey, are you gonna wish for a little lady friend to keep you company after I'm gone? I'm picturing a mouse—called Cat of course. Maybe she even carries a tiny little umbrella! Now how dandy would that be?"

He sharply deflected my question. "Lenny, point us in the direction of the wish basin. Let's get this over with."

"Oh, you mean my Jacuzzi? Well, it's down yonder," Lenny jerked his chin over an amber hill of the moon. "Don't be afraid to take a dip!"

"Well, come on then," Mouse growled, taking the lead. He was much grumpier than usual. I frowned. Was it something I said? He couldn't even be happy at a festival on the freaking moon! I made sure to give him a wide berth and floated behind as we trudged up the hill. Ahead of me, he hunched over in his raincoat and clenched his tiny paws.

After a long stretch of silence, we arrived at the basin. The pool was every bit as enchanting as Lenny had described.

An impossibly wide crater, hollow like a bowl, sat in the middle of the amber moon. It was filled to the brim with a strange kind of water I had never seen before: The elixir was a magnificent, shiny, milky white, glittering like a sea of stars. The whole thing was bathed in an ethereal glow.

When I looked to my right, I noticed a small sailboat that leaned against the wall of the basin.

Mouse saw it too, and his grouchy mood seemed to evaporate, if only for a moment. We shared a look that only two good friends could. He knew this was a journey I must make alone, and I knew he would be waiting for me on the other side of it. Awkwardly, he pulled out and handed me the bouquet of daisies I'd picked at the lake. I'd forgotten all about them.

"I thought you said they were sappy," I said.

"Well, you need all the help you can get."

"Any advice?"

He shrugged. "Don't trip. And think before you sneeze." And with that, he took off back toward the festival.

With a great heave, I pushed the sailboat. It tipped over the wall of the crater and splashed into the pool. I floated to it and settled into the snug ship. It slowly started to glide across the pool on its own.

As the current carried me forward, I looked down at the water. It was mesmerizing. I felt a strange pull on my heart, like the magic of the water was reaching out to me. And for the briefest moment, it was no longer a shimmering, milky white. It was all colors at once. I saw pinkish streaks of light, swirls of bright yellow, the hazy hue of green, and a flash of red.

Strange.

Not knowing what else to do, I squeezed my eyes shut and wished for the girl with sun-soaked hair and freckles like dirt.

When I opened my eyes, it was as if I'd drifted far away into an ocean. The crater was so vast and silent, far off from the noise of the festival. Out here, it was just me and my quiet heart.

Maybe she wasn't coming. Maybe she didn't want to see me.

After all, who was I? I didn't even have hair.

Just then, squinting into the distance, I made out a tiny blot of green. When the sailboat pushed further, it came into focus, and I could make out what it was.

And then I sneezed once, and I sneezed again, and then I probably sneezed three or four more times.

CHAPTER SIX
FRANKY

There was an island, but more importantly, there was a girl on the island.

Francine was exactly as I remembered her: Her blonde hair was barely contained in her misshapen braid. She was dressed in pink pajamas and missing one very important front tooth from her smile. I saw her notice my boat in the distance.

"Charlie!" She jumped up and down, waving.

I looked behind my shoulder. How could anyone have possibly followed me into the water basin? And where were their manners? Can't a sheet ghost be left alone for two seconds to remember the entirety of his existence?

Then it dawned on me. She was calling to me. Charlie.

"Charlie," I repeated, tasting the name in my mouth. It felt foreign but somehow strangely familiar, like a song whose rhythm I had known my whole life but was just now learning the lyrics to.

I tried to calm my breathing as my boat approached the green island. In one last frantic attempt, I tried to wiggle out the wrinkles in my sheet. I started to give myself a pep talk: *Hey, just because you don't have fluffy hair, and you're covered in daisies, doesn't make you any less of a stud.*

When my boat docked on the shore, she ran over to me in a quick blur of pink. She crashed into me, giving me a sheet-crushing hug.

"Oh, um, hello," I said, startled. Her golden hair itched my linen, but I didn't mind. She smelled like honey and freshly-baked biscuits.

"It's really you! I can't believe it!" she yelled, buried in my sheet.

She pulled back and looked at me so intensely that I felt quite wobbly. Her blue-gray eyes stared into the black holes where my eyes should be. My sheet started to feel very warm.

"How . . . How did you know it was me?" I asked.

Francine quirked her head, giggled, and tugged on my sheet. "When you got closer, I saw this ratty thing. I'd know it anywhere. Your bedroom sheets were hand-me-downs from your older sister. Boy," she hollered, "did you hate them! Always yapping about how they weren't manly enough for you."

"Oh." I sneezed. "Yeah, well, I'm—I'm much more mature now, so."

I felt like I was learning to use my voice for the very first time. Had it always been this high and squeaky?

"I'm sure." She laughed. It made something glow inside my heart.

Already, the pieces of my past were making me queasy. I looked down at my daisy flower sheet and felt a wave of warmth overtake me. A hand-me-down . . . from my older sister. I had an older sister! And that must mean I had a mother and a father too! Of course, I always did, but it never felt quite real until now. Learning this felt like when Mouse first gave me my nickname, only a thousand times better.

I made a vow right then and there to never complain about my flower sheet ever again. I would wear my hand-me-down like a badge of honor.

Suddenly, the bunches of flowers I was holding tickled my sheet. I shoved them into her hands. "These are for you."

She took them and held them up to her nose. "Thanks. Daisies are my favorite."

I shuffled in my sheet. "So—um . . . " I breathed. "How would you like to go to a festival on the moon with me?"

Francine smiled wide in agreement, proudly showing off her missing tooth.

❊ ❊ ❊

"And who's your li'l lady friend over here, Ghosty?" Lenny asked with a mischievous, knowing grin.

After about a million rides on the Ferris wheel, Francine and I stopped in line at one of the main tents, waiting for another round of sweets. Moonpies, it appeared, were not something easily acquired in the human world. Francine seemed to be keenly aware of this as she shoveled pies into her mouth as if she were preparing for hibernation.

"Um—well, she's not. She's, well, fascinating question you ask—"

Francine saved me from my blubbery. "I'm Franky."

"Yeah, she's Franky. And she's my—"

"Neighbor," she mumbled, cheeks stuffed to the brim with moonpies.

I gasped for air. "She's my neighbor."

"Well, he's actually always had a huge crush on me," she pointed out, matter-of-factly. "Left me little love notes everywhere and followed me around like a puppy. But I wanted to keep things

37

between us strictly platonic. Couldn't have my neighbor going all moony-eyed over me."

My sheet burned like fire as Lenny hooted and hollered. "That sounds 'bout right. I know what it's like to shoo away my fair amount of suitors."

In between bites of moonpie, Franky filled me in on the details from my past life. She lived in a brick house right across from mine on Becker Street. I had a mom, a dad, and a sister, Sally. I was eleven years old, and she was nine months older (she was very clear that that distinction mattered). She had confirmed that my hair was, in fact, brown and very fluffy.

Next to me, Mouse, who had been reluctantly trailing behind us during the festivities, huffed out.

"Got something to say back there, pip-squeak?" she asked.

The collective gasp Lenny and I made could probably be heard across the moon.

Frantically, I glanced at my furry friend. Oh my goodness—I was going to have to put myself in between them. He was going to shred my sheet in half!

But to my relief, Mouse only looked stunned, not provoked. Maybe even a little delighted at Franky's fire that could rival his own. "Just wondering what your outfit is all about."

"You guys don't have pajamas around here?"

"Well, of course we have pajamas," Lenny interjected. "I bet Mr. Mouse is just curious why you've decided to wear them here to the festival. Some of us like to dress with class," he retorted, tightening the bow tie around his neck.

Franky's eyes widened. "Oh that. Yeah, I don't know. I was sleeping, and then I just woke up on the island, like this is all a very strange, wonderful dream."

"Interesting, very interesting," Lenny added like it was some sort of detective case he was going to get to the bottom of. "And you came all the way here to see our li'l ghost friend. How nice and sweet and not at all romantic—"

"Lenny!" I squawked, sneezing.

Franky was unbothered by his teasing. "Bless you."

I stared at her. "What did you just say?"

"I blessed you. 'Cause you just sneezed. Why are you looking at me so funny?"

I looked back at Mouse. "Why have you never blessed me before?"

"Cats don't waste time with things like that."

Franky then talked out of the side of her mouth. "Speaking of weird outfits, what's the situation with the raincoat?"

"You know, no one really knows—"

Mouse must have overheard us and dramatically sighed. "Cats don't like water."

"Okay." She nodded. "But we're on the moon."

"Cats don't like the chance of water."

Franky's reply was cut off when we reached the stage with the woodland band. Her eyes lit up. To Lenny's absolute horror, she dropped her moonpie on the ground.

"Charlie! Let's dance!" She squealed, tugging on my sheet wildly.

"Oh," I blubbered, fighting the itch to sneeze. "Um—I don't really do that particular thing very well—"

But she was already pulling me by the corner of my sheet into the middle of the dance circle before I could finish my sentence. I watched as Lenny lifted Mouse onto his great shoulders in a way the bear would undoubtedly pay for later.

The air was thick with joy as creatures stomped and hollered to the rhythm of the music. Gnomes, scarecrows, and squirrels weaved in and out of the circle.

I stumbled, trying to remember my footing, which, of course, I didn't have. A brassy meow interrupted me from my panic. Above, a murderous Mouse was being heaved back and forth between all the bears like a beach ball, and I couldn't help but laugh.

I marveled at the wonder in front of me. The sound of folk music and the smell of cinnamon filled me up.

It was pure magic.

Then I saw Franky, pink in the cheeks, giggling as she spun with her arm out. She wobbled on the bouncy texture of the moon, and her honey hair blurred like streaks across its orange surface.

Then, very slowly, the music started to drift away. Around me, the crowd faded into the background. I only saw the girl twirling on the Harvest Moon.

All of a sudden, it was like the image of Franky had broken through the dam of memories in my mind. In a flash of light, everything came rushing to the surface. The force of impact was almost too much to withstand. I squeezed my eyes shut.

And I remembered.

CHAPTER SEVEN
THE SWEETEST APPLE

"Charlie, get your butt down here!" Franky called from below the apple tree, hands on her hips. Hot steam might as well have been shooting from her ears.

I ignored her and kept climbing, gripping the bark until my hands turned pink. I swung a skinny leg over a thick branch, trying to fit one dirty tennis shoe like a puzzle piece into the tree hollow. The traction didn't give, and I felt the sole of my shoe slipping. Quickly, I grabbed a branch from above to stabilize myself.

I heard a gasp from below. Through the thick leaves, I saw Franky cover her eyes with both hands.

"I mean it, you slug!" she yelled. "This is the dumbest thing you've ever done!"

"You said you wanted the best one," I shouted back, hoping she couldn't detect the fear laced through my voice. Tall heights were, admittedly, not my thing. "Everybody knows they're always at the top!"

"That wasn't an invitation for you to go up and grab it. You're clumsy on a good day!"

I turned back around, took a deep breath, and stood up to balance on the thickest branch. Through the leaves, I spotted my target: a ripe, bright red apple. Slowly, I stretched an arm out to it. My fingers had only just wrapped around the fruit when my knees wobbled, and my feet stumbled on the branch. I tumbled through the tree and landed on the ground with a loud smack.

Franky came flying over in an instant and kneeled next to me. "Oh my goodness, Charlie! Are you okay?"

A sharp, hot pain seared through my left arm, and tears blurred my shaky vision.

"Talk to me!" Franky called, tears streaming down her own freckled face.

I produced a small smile despite the throbbing. With my limp hand, I slowly lifted the apple I managed to rescue. Miraculously, it had survived the fall.

"Sweetest apple of the bunch, as requested."

Franky showed her gratitude by delivering a swift punch to my right arm.

"Ouch!" I yelped. "Try not to break my good arm, will you!"

When she helped me stand up, the ache was unbearable. I groaned as we made our way down the hill to her house.

"Well, go on," I gestured to the apple in her hand with a grunt. "Give it a taste."

She side-eyed me with flared nostrils. Reluctantly, she bit out of the honey crisp, and golden juice dribbled down her chin. A smile lit up her face before she could hide it. I knew it was one of the best things she'd ever eaten. Looking back at me, she simply shrugged. "It's alright."

Even through the pain, I managed to chuckle. "Liar! It was totally worth it!"

She furiously shook her head. "It was not!"

I looked at the pitiful sight of my already swelling arm and decided it was probably broken.

"You know, at least I'll get a cool cast. Everyone in the grade can sign it!"

My understanding of middle-grade currency was quick and fleeting, but I knew that having a cast to sign held a certain amount of credibility with sixth graders.

Franky whipped her head around to me. "They will do no such thing!"

"What do you mean?"

"If you do get a cast, you are not granted the luxury of getting it signed. You're going to write me an apology letter on it," she declared.

"A what?"

She nodded. "That way, every morning, you can read it and remember that you are never, ever allowed to scare me like that again."

Franky shot a stern look at me. She was a grade older and a head taller than me and she never, ever let me forget it. Bossing me around was her favorite pastime.

But even though she managed to smile, I could see the layer ofworry underneath and the tears that were still wet on her face. My fall had really rattled her.

"Hm. I'll think about it."

"That's if they don't have to amputate it," she added.

"They're not going to cut my arm off!" I yelled. Then paused. "Right?"

Another shrug. "We'll see."

Then she took another bite out of the apple, and the grin on her face made all the pain I felt disappear.

"I remember!" I shouted into the circle.

The Harvest Moon came back to me in a flash of orange light and a blend of instruments. The abruptness made me wobble, not to mention the weird looks I received from a family of scarecrows in front of me. But at the current moment, I couldn't be bothered to care.

"Franky!" I yelled, spinning around to search for her in the sea of dancers. She had her arms linked with Lenny, skipping around with him in the middle of the circle. I quickly pulled her away. She slumped down on top of a giant pumpkin nearby.

"The apple tree!" I blurted out. In my excitement, my words toppled over one another.

"What? I can't understand you!" she yelled over the music.

"The apple tree!" I screamed back.

She shook her head. I leaned closer.

"Did I ever write you that apology note?"

She looked at me in confusion until her brain caught up. Then her mouth split into a smile.

"Every inch of your cast was covered in it. You even made me a paper hard copy for safekeeping," she screamed back and laughed.

My sheet felt light and warm, like I could float up to the stars and back. I was dizzy in happiness, dizzy in bewilderment. Kind of just dizzy in general. *Man, I really need to start packing that Dramamine.*

I had a name. A family. A Franky!

My mind began to swirl with images from my life. I saw an older woman, my mother, and her eyes that crinkled in the sunlight. When I was younger, she sang me a soft lullaby to help me fall asleep. I saw my father with his calloused hands and warm smile and my sister, Sally, who always wore blue jean cutoffs. I saw all of us together in a too-small house that was always cluttered with laundry and the smell of oatmeal cookies.

It was like I was seeing colors for the very first time.

I looked down to ask Franky more questions but noticed she had gone really quiet. She was picking at the lint on her pajamas, her feet dangling off the pumpkin.

"Franky?" I said. What could have gone wrong so quickly? I finally remembered her! I thought she would be jumping up and down.

She didn't respond to me. Instead, she clicked together her fuzzy bedtime slippers.

"What's wrong?"

Finally, she glanced up.

"Do you . . . do you remember anything else about that day you broke your arm?"

Puzzled, I tried to wade through the foggy memories in my head but came up short. They were so jumbled together it felt like trying to float through sand.

"It's hard to tell . . . but no. I don't think so. Why?"

She took a deep breath. "Charlie, that was only a couple of days before you died."

The words weighed on me like a heavy blanket. Whatever I was expecting her to say, it certainly wasn't that.

For some reason, I had never given too much thought to when or how I died. I guess because it never really felt like *that* big of a deal. After all, I had just woken up here. And I had Mouse. So it wasn't like I just vanished out of nowhere.

"Oh, okay," I laughed anxiously, trying to dispel some of her worry. She was clearly shaken up about it, but I didn't want her to be. "So, um, well, how did it happen?"

She looked back down at her slippers. Why was she so apprehensive about telling me?

Oh god, I thought, *it was probably something horribly catastrophic.* Like an explosion caused by me. I gulped, suddenly remembering how I never bothered to figure out what was actually supposed to go in the microwave and what was not. What were the rules about tinfoil again? No idea. Yep, that's probably what did it. One pizza roll, and I flew too close to the sun.

I nodded frantically, bracing for the impact. "You can tell me. Even if it was really embarrassing. It's fine. I can take it."

Mouse and his bright yellow raincoat appeared out of absolutely nowhere. Apparently, he had managed to escape from the partying bears.

"I can all but guarantee it was embarrassing," he chimed in.

"Sorry, this conversation is only for people up to here," I quickly shouted back, stretching out my hand at my sheet's shoulder to a height far above Mouse's.

"Well, I'm just looking at the facts. You trip over your sheet on a daily basis. Quite impressively, might I add, given that you have no feet."

Death didn't matter that much to cats. I guess that's what happens when you get nine lives.

"Oh, and," Mouse said, redirecting his attention to Franky. "He, in fact, cannot take it. He is a walking ball of panic and anxiety, so please be gentle on him."

"No, it was nothing embarrassing," she said quietly. Her voice was soft, devoid of the spunk I'd learned to be her trademark.

"Okay." I swallowed. "So what was it?"

"It was an accident, Charlie. A really bad accident."

I sucked in a breath. Next to me, even Mouse seemed caught off guard in a way my sharp friend so rarely was.

"What kind of accident?" Mouse questioned.

Franky looked up at the stars. "I remember . . . I remember my mom saying that the car just came out of nowhere on the street," she let out. "When everyone got there, your bicycle was in five pieces."

A long moment of silence stretched out between the three of us. It's possible the entire moon could have gone still. I tried to form words, but they caught in the back of my throat.

I shut my eyes. Concentrating hard, I pulled on the strings of my memory, and all the images fit into place.

Suddenly, I was an eleven-year-old boy again, not a sheet ghost. I pedaled the wheels of my bike hard with my worn-out tennis shoes. The wind was flapping my hair through the holes in my helmet. On my left arm was a bright blue, extremely itchy cast. It was covered in wobbly handwriting addressed to Franky.

It all happened in a blur. The loud honk, the screeching of the tires. I tried to swerve out of the way, but the cast made my arm too stiff to squeeze the brakes. There wasn't enough time to reach over with my good arm.

And then, a blinding light and everything folded in on itself.

"It's all my fault," Franky stammered, breaking me out of my trance.

"What do you mean?" Mouse asked.

Franky looked directly at me. "It's because you had the cast."

Mouse shook his head. "I don't understand."

"He broke his arm falling out of the apple tree," Franky explained. "And you were only up there 'cause you wanted to get me the best apple."

"So when the car came . . . " Mouse began.

"You couldn't hit the brakes," Franky sniffled. "'Cause you're left-handed."

Too much was happening. All of the joy I felt moments before had been sucked out of the air. There were suddenly so many noises around me. The music drummed in my sheet, and the loud laughter of festivalgoers clouded my thoughts.

"Charlie, I'm so sorry!" she cried. The twinkle of the night sky reflected in her eyes.

I could barely process what she was saying. I tried to shut it out and drown the noise and the lights, but it was no use.

"I just—I need a minute," I muttered.

"No, Charlie, wait—" she shouted.

But it was too late. I had already floated off as fast as my sheet could take me.

CHAPTER EIGHT
ALL THE COLORS AT ONCE

❋ ❋ ❋

"Ghosty? Are you in there?" Mouse called.

The thing about sneezing when you're a sheet ghost is that things could go terribly wrong when you hold it in. I've always imagined the air from the sneeze shooting up into my sheet like a bomb, and then it blows the whole thing off. One thing I knew was that I really did *not* want to see what was under my floral sheet. That was an existential crisis I was not equipped to deal with.

So when I sneezed underneath the seat of the Ferris wheel's cabin while it was temporarily stalled, I blew my own cover.

"Now, I only know one sheet ghost who sneezes when he's upset. So you can come out now."

"Just leave me alone," I yelled back.

"No can do. You're my ride," Mouse said, sliding into the seat. I reluctantly floated up from under my hiding spot and joined him. He reached over and pulled the lever in front of our legs.

As the Ferris wheel jolted and started to rise, we sat in silence.

I looked out at the festival until everything became a blur of golden light. My hazy vision focused on the soft horizon past the hills and craters. We must've been up here for a while, I realized, as the sky had started to lighten. The sun was waking up.

"I never got to grow out of my sneakers," I said softly. My mind was elsewhere, thinking about the beat-up white tennis shoes I had climbed the apple tree with. I knew it was silly to focus on something so small in the wake of everything. But I couldn't stop thinking about their frayed shoelaces, how torn the soles were, and the huge hole in the left heel. My mom had promised me new ones for my twelfth birthday.

I remembered it was supposed to be space themed. Ever since I was a little boy, I wanted to be an astronaut. My dad even plastered glow-in-the-dark stars all along the ceiling of my bedroom for me. At night, I would jump on my bed and pretend I was drifting into the cosmos.

"You know, it's funny," I began. "I didn't ever really think about my death because it never occurred to me that I had so much to leave behind. But I had a life, Mouse. I had a mom, a dad, and a sister, and Franky was there, too. And now it's all . . . gone."

It was an ache like I had never known. The feeling was murky to wade through because, on some level, I knew how lucky I was. I thought about the sad sheet ghost at the edge of the moon. They had no idea who they were and no recollection of the life they lived. But me, well, all I wanted was to come to the moon and figure out why I kept seeing Franky. Instead, I got even more than I wished for. I gained a family, a name, a friend. But it was all ripped away from me in the same second.

Mouse didn't say anything to me, clearly at a loss for words, and I didn't blame him. I felt bad for putting him in this spot

because I knew how much he hated dealing with emotions. But I pushed on because there was one thing that had been gnawing at the back of my mind.

"When Franky was talking about the accident, I remembered everything that happened. The bike . . . the car . . . and something else. I just couldn't bring myself to say it in front of Franky. Too weird to tell her."

"What was it?"

"Right after I died, I think I saw her. I think she was the last thing I saw before I came here. Everything was blurry, but I knew it was her because when she smiled, she was missing her front tooth. Anyway, she reached for my hand, and we walked toward this warm, fuzzy kind of light . . . " I trailed off.

I looked out again. In the quietness of all quiet, I began to think that the condition of being a sheet ghost is not entirely unlike that of the moon. Not the Harvest Moon—the beautiful and brilliant one that people wait the whole year to celebrate. But the lonely moon that spends its days rising and falling, waiting for the sun it will never get to see.

And I finally understood why us sheet ghosts wake up here without any memories. It was easier that way. Because if we all knew what we had said goodbye to, we would spend the rest of our days waiting for the sun that would never rise again. Always mourning all that we had and all that we lost.

I couldn't take it. Turning to Mouse abruptly, I shouted, "I wish I didn't remember anything!"

He shook his head. "Surely you don't mean that."

"I do, Mouse! It's not fair. I wish I could forget all of this. It was better before."

He thought about that for a while. When we reached the peak of the Ferris wheel, we looked down below us. A scene unfolded as the crowd below released a sea of round, glowing lanterns. The big finale. They floated high in the sky, blending in with the disappearing stars.

"I'm not sure," Mouse spoke finally. "But I think you are on to something, my friend. Is it so bad to remember the people we love, even if it hurts a little?"

Then he shrugged, and the hood of his raincoat flapped above his eyes. "And, well, how lucky is that? That death is only your childhood best friend waiting to hold your hand."

Before I could think more about what he said, a strange flash of color in the distance caught my eye. I'd almost forgotten about the wishing well.

Even from all the way up at the Ferris wheel, I could see that strange swirl of colors again in the pool—the pinkish streaks and the glowing ripples of yellow. The odd blend of red and green.

Then I looked back at Mouse, and I was struck by the very specific, squeaky yellow of his raincoat. And then thought back to the pale pink of Franky's pinstripe pajamas. The green leaves in the tree and the bright red of the apple.

All the colors at once.

How peculiar, I thought. *Why would the basin show me Mouse and Franky?*

Then, the Ferris wheel started to sink back to the ground. I gazed over at Mouse, who was looking back at me with wide, green eyes.

"When'd you get so wise?"

"It's the whole nine lives thing. You're bound to learn a lesson or two."

I nodded. "I'm not sure I can say goodbye to her."

"Well, I suppose we could just ride the Ferris wheel forever. That is, until Lenny runs out of moonpies and tries to eat us."

"Funny."

"And we've got your sheet ghost Dramamine shortage to worry about. Plus, there's a very emotional, distraught little girl down there that I would rather not have to deal with, so maybe it's for the best."

I laughed, then said, "Mouse?"

"Hm?"

I started to form the words of a thank you, but that didn't feel big enough.

"Nothing, I—just—You're my best friend."

"Well, that I knew."

CHAPTER NINE
GOODBYE

When Mouse and I walked back toward the festival, all the vendors were starting to pack up the tents. Most of the crowd had dissipated, departing from the moon on their various modes of transportation. I looked for Lenny, pitying the soul who was going to have to tell him the celebration was wrapping up. I found him on the stage, where it appeared that he and his uncle Rick had mended their broken past to belt out one last encore with the band.

"Goodnight everybody!" Lenny hollered. "And just remember, you can take the bear out of the party, but you can't take the party of the bear! See y'all next year!"

We found Franky off to the side, absentmindedly picking at the pieces of a moonpie. She saw us and started to walk over hesitantly.

"I'll give you two a moment," Mouse said and slipped off into what was left of the festival.

Franky reached me and stared at her slippers. Then she mumbled, "I wasn't sure I should stay to say goodbye."

"What?" I asked.

"Oh," she sighed. "You're upset at me, right? I mean, you have every right to be."

"What are you talking about?"

"Well, it's all my fault, isn't it?" She let out. "If you hadn't broken your arm, you would have been able to swerve out of the way. None of it would've happened! You must hate me."

I finally caught up, recalling our last conversation before I took off for the Ferris wheel. Oh goodness, I had been so dense. All of her feelings had completely gone over my sheet. I hadn't realized she blamed herself.

"Oh Franky. There are probably about a million rules saying you can't ride a bike with a cast on. Really, it's my fault. I can be so dumb sometimes."

"But you only had the cast 'cause you wanted to get me the sweetest apple! Gosh, you have no idea how guilty I've felt!"

I pushed on, trying to get her to see my reasoning. "What do you mean guilty? Franky, you have nothing to be sorry for!"

She buried her face in her hands and sobbed, collapsing down against the pumpkin. Not knowing what to do, I floated down to be level with her.

"Um," I glanced around frantically, searching for a tissue to stop her tears. None in sight. I guess they don't carry Kleenex on the moon.

"Er, here you go," I said, awkwardly nudging her toward my sheet.

It drew a small, soft laugh out of Franky. She grabbed a handful of my sheet in her fist and blew her nose in it. "Thanks."

"Anytime," I said, slouching.

Neither of us spoke for a while. We listened to the soft hum of the music from the stage and the chattering of the last few festivalgoers leaving the moon.

Finally, she looked at me with watery eyes. "I see you all the time in my dreams, Charlie."

"What do you mean?"

"I'm . . . I'm always looking for you there. We're right back at the apple tree, and if I can just get you down before you fall, I know I will save you. But I never can."

I perked up in my sheet. "You've been dreaming about the apple tree?"

She nodded, sniffling with her stuffy nose. "Yeah, why?"

I thought back to all the times I had gotten a strange flashback to the girl with the apple tree. The golden hue of her hair, the blend of red and green. Like a murky dream.

What if Franky had been dreaming about me and the apple tree in her world all this time? Was that how I remembered her? It didn't make any sense, but did that mean it was impossible?

"I think . . . I think that's how I remembered you, Franky," I said.

"Huh?"

"Somehow, you contacted me through your dreams. Ever since I came to this world, I kept getting these visions of you and the apple tree. I think that must've been every time you dreamed about me."

Franky considered that, scrunching her nose. I hadn't really noticed how young she looked until then. Barely thirteen-years-old, she was just a girl.

Yet it was like her sadness had swallowed her whole. It had been powerful enough to somehow transcend the fabric of her world and reach me here. No matter how tough she pretended to be, I could tell that she had been carrying the grief of losing her friend for so long.

And I needed her to know it was okay to let go.

"You can forgive yourself, alright?"

She jerked her head quickly. Always so stubborn. "Never."

"No, I mean it. Look," I took a breath. "I was always going to get you that apple, okay? There was no getting around it. Even in your dreams, you can try every which way not to get me to climb up, but I'm always gonna. Because . . . well, there's never going to be a universe where I don't want to make you smile."

She pulled her legs tight to her chest and hugged them, propping her chin on her knees. "I just can't believe you're gone."

I nodded. "I know . . . but I think I'm going to be okay here. Plus, you know, we have moonpies. Can't beat that."

She chuckled, wiping her nose. "I suppose so."

"Yeah, so don't worry."

Franky took a deep breath and released it. "Okay," she sniffled. Then she fixed me with an intense stare. "I'm never going to forget about you, Charlie. Never, ever."

She furrowed her brows and tightened her lips. I was struck by her determination. It seemed like it was not only a promise to me, but to the moon, the stars, and maybe even the whole universe. The resolve in her voice sounded like a challenge to anything that dared to get in the way of it. Like she was bating time, old age, and maybe even death itself to try to prevent her from remembering me.

"I'll never forget you either," I said.

And I meant it. I thought back to the basin. The strange swirl of shades and hues. Mouse, Franky, the apple tree. Then I started to think about how none of this would mean anything without those memories. It's the people we love who make life all colors at once. And how could I ever not want to remember them?

Franky smiled back at me, missing tooth and all.

"You better not, slug."

We found ourselves back at the edge of the water basin. Franky hugged me like we were two colliding stars as dawn kissed the horizon.

"It's not fair," she murmured into my sheet. "I just got you back."

I breathed in her smell one last time: biscuits, honey, and home.

"We'll see each other again," I told her. After all, I had enough Harvest Moon wishes to spare.

She bobbed her head up and down quickly, wiping away a remaining tear. "Same time next year?"

"Same time next year," I repeated. Then, "Oh and Franky?"

"Hm?"

"Is . . . Is my family okay?"

She gave me a smile. "They are. I mean, everyone misses you a whole lot. But they're okay."

I felt a wave of relief wash over my sheet. "Look after them for me, will you?"

"Yeah, I will."

Then she turned on her heels and put her hands on her hips. All business. She eyed Mouse, who had just sauntered up to join us. "You take care of him, okay? We both know he's too delicate to be a sheet ghost in the wild."

The tabby did not like to be bossed around, especially by a thirteen-year-old. "Alright, alright, little girl. Don't you have a magical island to get back to?"

Franky clutched the crumpled bouquet of daisies to her chest, gave me one last look, and then plopped down in the boat.

"So long, you two," she called and tipped an imaginary sailor's hat in our direction.

Mouse and I pushed the boat off the surface and into the pool. It slowly started to float into the abyss. We watched it for a long time until it disappeared into the still water. The last thing I saw was the golden hue of her hair.

Goodbye, Franky.

When I looked back to the edge of the basin, I was surprised to see another sailboat had taken its place. It was propped up against the crater like an invitation.

Mouse was clearly bothered by this new addition, but I wasn't sure why. He shoved two paws in his raincoat.

"I guess this is goodbye for us, too." He muttered, nearly inaudible.

I tilted the top of my sheet at him. "What do you mean?"

"Well, I just figured you'd be on your way out now that you don't have anything weighing you down."

I hadn't even thought about that. But technically, he was right. Now that I remembered my past, nothing was holding me back. I finally had the freedom to leave this world, to find my peace. After all, that's what a sheet ghost was supposed to do, right?

"I wouldn't even know how to do that," I replied.

He nodded his head in the direction of the sailboat that had appeared. "I'm willing to bet that magical pool over there will take you anywhere you want to go."

Then he kicked a pebble of the moon with his foot, refusing to meet my gaze. Something about how sullen he looked made me think back to earlier when we had first encountered the moon pool. He was so crotchety when I left to make my wish, especially when I mentioned leaving. I had chalked it up to his normal moodiness, but had there been a deeper reason?

"Mouse?"

"Hm?" He pouted, whiskers downturned. The hood of his raincoat had fallen off his tiny head.

"Is that why you were so grumpy earlier? You thought I was going to leave all this behind?"

"Well, don't you want to?"

"I . . . I don't know."

"You could find your peace, Ghosty," he said with a sad look.

I glanced out to the basin of water. What did peace even mean? I pictured the sailboat carrying me far off into the distance, past the island. I wondered if it would be like slowly drifting off to sleep. Would I hear my mother's lullaby again?

Despite everything, it might be easier, in some ways. If I left this place behind, I wouldn't have to carry all that I had lost with me. There wouldn't be any pain to remember.

I wondered if that was what I wanted.

Could I really say goodbye to all of this?

Then I looked back at my friend in the yellow raincoat. And, suddenly, the weight of everything seemed a little easier to bear.

I knew there was only one real choice.

"Yeah." I cleared my throat. "I mean, I could do that."

He slumped his shoulders.

"But . . . " I dragged out. "You know, what's the rush? I could wait around for another life. Maybe even two."

Mouse lifted his chin and his ears perked up. "What?"

"Yeah," I said, shrugging. "I think I'll stick around for a bit. You know, at least until you finally kick the bucket."

He forced a sigh, but even he couldn't disguise his appeasement. "That is some extremely sensitive information you're sitting on."

The two of us exchanged an awkward look. What were we supposed to do now? Hug? I was pretty sure that was uncharted emotional territory for Mouse. How does a sheet ghost even hug a cat?

Then, I realized something. "Wait! Your wish. You haven't made one yet!"

"Oh," Mouse chided. "Don't worry about that."

I had already spun around and started to float toward the basin. "C'mon, we're right here."

Mouse didn't budge an inch. "It's fine."

"You gotta make a wish on the Harvest Moon!"

"Ghosty, come back. I already made one."

"What? When?" I asked.

"When you and Franky were having your touching little heart-to-heart after the Ferris wheel."

I thought back to it. I remembered him slipping off, but I had just assumed it was to pull Lenny from the stage.

"Oh, okay," I responded. "Wait, so what did you wish for?"

He quickly shook his head. "Not important."

"C'mon, tell me!"

He sighed long and dramatically like he had a deep, deep pain. "Well, if you simply must know, after our conversation, I was thinking about the logistics of everything. You know, me being a cat with two lives left and you a sheet ghost. I figured it wouldn't be bad to get some insurance in case you did decide to stay."

"And?"

"And . . . well, I just wished that we would be friends." He coughed. "Forever." Rolled his eyes. "So we won't get separated."

Warmth swelled inside my sheet. "Mouse, you old softy."

"Yeah, yeah," he mumbled, stalking back to the festival.

I floated right beside him.

"So . . ."

"What, Ghosty?"

"What was your original wish going to be?"

"Oh that," he said with a dismissive wave of his paw. "I got cursed to be followed by an invisible storm cloud wherever I go. I've been trying to get rid of it for some time now. It is truly quite cumbersome."

"What?" I asked, absolutely flabbergasted. "When on earth did that happen?"

He thought to himself. "Somewhere around life four, I believe. Hence the raincoat."

"Wow."

"Looks like I'll be stuck with it for another year, at least."

I shook my head. "You can't just keep dropping random, life-altering things that happened in your past lives on me. One of these days, we've really got to sit down with a timeline."

Mouse shrugged. "Seems like we've got all the time in the world for that."

"That and about an infinite amount of Lenny's parties to attend."

"Oh god," Mouse groaned. "Speaking of that bear, let's go find him before he gets bored and tries to turn those goldfish into a birthday cake."

I laughed. "Lead the way."

And together, Mouse and I walked around the Harvest Moon and back again.

ACKNOWLEDGMENTS

To Sara, Meg, and all of Wilde Press, *thank you, thank you, thank you*. You have given me the greatest gift by bringing my silly little story to life. Knowing how much work was put into this project, specifically by the substantive, copyediting, and design teams, makes my heart glow. I want to especially thank Maggie, whose hand probably still hurts from how tightly I held onto it throughout the editorial process. Someone should maybe check on her.

I owe so much to so many people. I'll begin with my mom, who has never let me quit a single thing in my life, even when I kicked and screamed. If she hadn't taught me perseverance, then the first draft of this would have never been written. And my dad, whose ridiculous love of Dungeons and Dragons and knack for storytelling has made this book what it is (in more ways than one). More importantly, he has made me who I am (in more ways than one).

To Grandmama Avis, for always being my first reader. Mimi, my biggest cheerleader (and who, if moonpies from the Harvest Moon really did exist, could undoubtedly bake the best one). And Mickey, my 102-year-old great-grandmother, who gave me my love of books. Also to Bob, for all the advice he gives me because even though I never really ask for any of it, it's often very good.

I also wanted to thank Dev for many things but mostly for taking care of me throughout these past months of writing. Lastly, Sophia, my roommate, who didn't complain when I held her hostage in my bedroom and forced her to read Lenny's dialogue in a Southern accent. And because, well, if I hadn't met her, then I would never have been able to write a book about how magical friendships can be.

There are so many others: Professor Lise Haines, Rhyne, Kelly, Kasen, Hailey, Oliver, the list goes on.

Thank you!

Photo by Abigail Dare Oliver

Callan Whitley is from New Bern, North Carolina. She loves tea, rainy days, blankets fresh out of the laundry, and oatmeal cookies. She is studying Writing, Literature, and Publishing at Emerson College in the great city of Boston. One day, she hopes to escape to a cottage in the middle of nowhere in Scotland with a whole bunch of books and probably a dog.

Publisher

Sara Fergang

Editorial Department

Head Editor

Maggie Keating

Assistant Editor

Samantha Kavich

Associate Editors

Ali Denning ✸ Pia LaPlaca ✸ Eva Windler ✸ Emma Winiarski

Production Department

Proofreader

Liz Gómez

Head Copyeditor

Ella Maoz

Assistant Copyeditor

Kyndle Fuller

Associate Copyeditors

Meg Carey ✸ Shannon Cullen ✸ Deb Fahel ✸ Ari LaColla ✸
Isabelle McMahan ✸ Ella Miller ✸ Anna Scarpone

Associate Publisher

Amber Heaney

Marketing Department

Marketing Head

Joei Chan

Marketing Assistant

Sally Beckett

Associate Marketers

Shannon Cullen ❀ Liberty Henry ❀ Reid Perry ❀ Rebecca Verrill

Design Department

Art Director

Anya Getschel

Design Manager

Meg Carey

Design Assistant

Allie Montenegro

Associate Designers

Isabella Chiu ❀ Elisabeth Grass ❀ Ella Mastroianni ❀
Isabelle McMahan ❀ Eva Windler

www.ingramcontent.com/pod-product-compliance
Lightning Source LLC
Chambersburg PA
CBHW012019110726
47994CB00009B/3225